W9-AHL-628

# TURTLE TUBE

## An Erutuf National Park Novel

Kathy Arnold Cherry

ARCHWAY
PUBLISHING

Copyright © 2021 Kathy Arnold Cherry.

All rights reserved. No part of this book may be used or reproduced by any means, graphic, electronic, or mechanical, including photocopying, recording, taping or by any information storage retrieval system without the written permission of the author except in the case of brief quotations embodied in critical articles and reviews.

This is a work of fiction. All of the characters, names, incidents, organizations, and dialogue in this novel are either the products of the author's imagination or are used fictitiously.

Archway Publishing books may be ordered through booksellers or by contacting:

Archway Publishing
1663 Liberty Drive
Bloomington, IN 47403
www.archwaypublishing.com
844-669-3957

Because of the dynamic nature of the Internet, any web addresses or links contained in this book may have changed since publication and may no longer be valid. The views expressed in this work are solely those of the author and do not necessarily reflect the views of the publisher, and the publisher hereby disclaims any responsibility for them.

Any people depicted in stock imagery provided by Getty Images are models, and such images are being used for illustrative purposes only. Certain stock imagery © Getty Images.

ISBN: 978-1-6657-1056-5 (sc)
ISBN: 978-1-6657-1054-1 (hc)
ISBN: 978-1-6657-1055-8 (e)

Library of Congress Control Number: 2021915489

Print information available on the last page.

Archway Publishing rev. date: 08/17/2021

To Carter and Kaitlyn for sparking magic
And to Steve for inspiring adventure

# Contents

# Erutuf

# The Home Page

The website's home page stares back. Reese looks up at options and options of videos. They all shout silently, "Pick me, play me." Trending, subscriptions, originals, and favorites all await the big selection. She scrolls slowly down the home page.

"Reese, which one are you watching tonight? I'm watching the sports guys' videos again," says Dean, her younger eight-year-old brother. He doesn't look up from his tablet, which is technically Mom's old tablet.

"I'm still looking," ten-year-old Reese replies while scrolling on her tablet.

Reese and Dean Walters love to watch videos online like many of their friends. This particular website has endless options. They can watch tons of videos on animals, video games, toys, clothing, hairstyles, sports, and many other topics. Each video offers suggestions to other related videos. If their parents allowed it, they could watch videos for hours and hours.

"Have you seen the funny one with the puppy trying to climb up stairs for the first time? That puppy is so funny!" Dean asks. He sees his sister still trying to pick out a video.

Reese replies, "I think so. I am looking for a video on turtles right now." She doesn't take her eyes off the tablet.

"Haven't you seen them all yet?" Dean asks. Reese rolls her eyes at him in response. He knows how much Reese loves sea turtles, and she usually watches turtle videos or animal videos. Reese can't wait to get older. She wants to become a marine biologist and help save sea turtles and other living creatures in the oceans.

From the sofa, she takes a minute to stretch out her arms and flip over to lie down on her belly. Their golden retriever, Tutu, takes this movement as an invitation to hop up on the other end of the sofa and curl up. Reese named Tutu about six years ago, when Reese was only four years old. She wanted the name Turtle, but Dean couldn't say that word quite yet, being only two years old. Therefore, Turtle became Tutu. Reese also wonders if her parents didn't want their dog called another animal's name. Tutu fits her because she has a ballerina-like grace. And Tutu loves to snuggle both of them; she would make it her full-time job if she could.

"I think I found a new sea-turtle video by a new person, Dean. Do you want to watch this one with me?" Reese asks. She knows he likes to watch these turtle videos more than he will admit. Reese knows she can't tell his friends that he watches sea-turtle videos with her—he would be so embarrassed!

"Sure, I am almost done with this video. Maybe this sea turtle will poop in the video," Dean replies, smiling back at his sister.

Reese shakes her head slightly. As she waits for him to finish his own video, she loads hers up so it will be ready to watch. The video is not too long. Reese is getting more excited to see this new one. A new person uploaded this video, and it looks like it is his or her first video. Their channel name is Turtle Tube, which makes her giggle. Reese loves to find new turtle people to follow and will be one of their first subscribers. She quickly hits subscribe and is now signed up to follow them.

"Are you done yet? I'm ready to watch it," Reese says. She rubs her hand along her long brown ponytail and moves back into a sitting position.

"What did the beach say to when the tide came in? Long time, no sea!" Dean says, falling over while laughing.

Reese rolls her eyes and quickly hides her smile. "Oh, you and your silly jokes! I guess you're ready. I'm starting the video. Come over here."

"You love my jokes! I'm coming. Who is this person?" Dean says. He squeezes into a small spot between Reese and the oversized arm of the gray sofa.

"Really? You have to sit there? Anyway, it's Turtle Tube, and this is their first video," she answers. Dean giggles at the name, and Reese can't help but giggle with him. Tutu scoots closer to the two siblings. "There's no description about this video, but let's watch it! Let's go, Turtle Tube!" Reese says as she hits the play button.

The video starts off quiet, with pretty ballet music playing in the background. Blue ocean water fills the tablet screen. Little fish start swimming toward the center of the camera. In the distance, a small head appears to swim slowly. The sea turtle moves closer, gliding along with the music. No one has said anything in the video yet. This sea turtle glides with the music as if she is dancing. Her front flippers move to the music. Her head turns toward the camera, and her big, calm eyes stare into the camera.

Dean and Reese watch this sea turtle glide around to the music. She is so majestic and graceful. Neither of them speak to each other. They can't keep their eyes off this video. The music, the ocean movements, the sea turtle glides, and the little fish fluttering around in the background hypnotize Dean and Reese. Tutu glances up at the screen and tilts her head to the music, her eyes tracking the turtle.

The video screen blinks a few times at Dean and Reese.

"What is going on?" Dean asks Reese.

Tutu hops off the sofa and heads into the kitchen, whining.

"I have no idea. Maybe if we wait a few minutes, it will restart," Reese replies.

The screen continues to blink in blue and green. The ballet music continues playing though through the blinks.

"How is the music playing if this video isn't going?" Reese asks.

"I don't know. I have never seen this happen in a video before," Dean responds.

The music gets louder without either of them pushing a button. Dean and Reese look at each other with big eyes. Reese pushes the button on her tablet to lower the music, but it only gets louder.

Dean reaches for her tablet at the same time she's still trying to fix the sound. Dean tugs on the left side of it, and Reese holds onto the right side. The music blares at the top level, and a poof of blueish green color appears in the air and swirls above them. The colors swirl around. After several seconds, Dean and Reese float up into the air and into the colors. They twirl around and around with the colors. The twirls feel like forever as the music plays on.

With a quiet bump, Dean and Reese land on a beach. The music has stopped, and the swirling colors have stopped. No one is around them.

# Erutuf National Park

"What just happened?" Dean shouts, jumping up from the soft sand.

"Where are we?" asks Reese. She stands slowly and dusts off the sand on her purple leggings.

The white sand sparkles all around Dean and Reese and reflects like stars in a night sky. It seems like someone painted the sky the prettiest blue color. Palm trees behind them wave in the wind. The waves on the water come in and out on the beach shorelines. They don't see any boats or another shoreline in the distance.

"Well, I think we are on a beach!" says Dean while staring at the water.

"Great one, brother!" replies Reese, turning around and looking behind them toward the trees.

"Hey, where do boats go when they are sick?" asks Dean. He grins and reaches down to touch some soft sand.

"Where?" Reese asks. She is looking for a boat somewhere out in the ocean.

"To the dock!" Dean answers, falling down on the sand and giggling like a hyena.

"Really? You are laughing while we are mysteriously placed on some random beach? We were just watching a video and landed somehow on a beach, and all you can do is tell one of your jokes and laugh," Reese scolds. She starts walking down the beach away from him. She knows he simply wants some attention, but she wants to focus on where they are.

"Hey, I just wanted to make you smile," Dean yells as he runs up to catch up to her.

"I am not smiling. I don't understand where we are right now. I have to figure this out—and watch you too."

"I'm not that much younger than you. And I can help figure this out too. I mean, it's kind of cool that we are standing on a beach somewhere," Dean says, reaching to hold Reese's hand.

She squeezes it softly. "You're right. I'm sorry I yelled at you. Let's figure this out as a team, like when we play games at home." She gives him a quick hug.

"I'll race you to the big shell up ahead!" Dean says.

"Okay, go!" Reese answers. They dash ahead to the large shell.

"I won! Hey, what kind of shell is this one? It's huge," Dean says while looking it over.

The shell sits in the sand. It could be a play structure at a park, but it's a real seashell hanging out on the beach. The cream and yellow colors sparkle on it.

"You beat me! And I don't know what kind of shell it is. Look, there are some people around those trees. Should we go talk to them?" Reese asks while pointing.

"Mom says that we shouldn't talk to strangers."

"Yes, but, we need a little help in figuring out where we are. They look like a regular family on a vacation. Let's not tell them that we are lost. I'll talk, and you just stay with me."

"Okay. I was hoping to make a sand fort first. I'm not doing any talking," Dean says.

"We can make sand forts later. Let's go. I'll talk." Reese takes her brother's thin hand into hers. Reese and Dean walk together toward the palm trees and the family while the ocean water crashes.

A tall man with a baseball hat and sunglasses waits for his wife and two girls following behind him. He places a large beach bag on the sandy ground under the palm tree. The woman stands at average height with long brown hair tucked under a large, floppy brown beach hat. The two girls look about five and two years old. The youngest girl's hair swings in long pigtails as she jogs to keep up with her mom and sister. The older sister talks and talks to her mom. Her mom waves to her husband to keep going and find a spot. He shakes his head no and waits.

Reese and Dean walk through the sand toward the family. Dean starts humming an Imagine Dragons song, and Reese joins in. Then Dean freezes and looks at his sister with his big brown eyes.

"What? Why did you stop?" Reese asks.

"What if it starts to thunder and lightning?" Dean asks, still standing frozen.

"It's a song, not happening here. Look at these blue skies," Reese replies.

"Not the song. What if it really storms here, and we are on a beach?" Dean says as he stomps his feet into the sand.

"We will be okay. I really don't think that we need to worry about a storm. We will be home before we need to worry about the weather. Let's keep walking and talk to this family," Reese reassures him, and she puts her arm around his shoulders. Dean leans into the hug and hopes his sister is right about the weather.

The woman and two girls reach the man. The dad lays out a large beach blanket. The mom takes some toys out of the bag. The girls each grab a toy and immediately start playing in the sand under the tree on the blanket. The tree provides a bit of umbrella coverage from the bright sun for the family.

As Dean and Reese come within a few feet of the family, the family settles into their environment. The girls play in the sand with their beach toys. The mom reads her latest book club novel. The dad games on his cell phone. No one in the family glances up at the two kids.

"Hello, can we ask you a few questions?" Reese asks while standing near the mom. The woman does not reply or even glance at them.

"Hello, family, can you hear us? We just have a couple of questions," Reese tries again while looking at Dean and then back at the family. The family continues to ignore them without looking at them or replying.

Dean jumps up and down by doing some jumping jacks and yells, "I'm a funny little boy!" The family does not notice or even blink.

"Dean, I'm not sure they see us," Reese says while rubbing her eyes.

"You think they are blind and maybe deaf?" Dean asks, dancing around his older sister to get some sort of response.

"No, they definitely aren't blind or deaf. We saw their movements and heard them before now. I don't understand. Maybe it's magic?" Reese replies.

Dean stops jumping. They both sit down on the sand and look at the family. Dean frowns at the sand.

"Jack, what do you think about this Erutuf National Park so far?" the woman says to her husband while resting her book on her lap and ending their silence.

"This national park has definitely lived up to the hype so far. The website called it America's ideal and now largest national park. I still can't believe the variety on this island in the Pacific Ocean. What you do think?" Jack replies while still gaming on his cell phone.

"I agree. I never thought I'd see something that made Yellowstone or Yosemite look small! The girls also seem to enjoy it, with all the variety in landscapes, animals, and programs offered here. I would love to know who donated all of this to the government! I am still amazed that in today's world, it is still a secret. The donor even built all the trails, visitor centers, lodges, restaurants, and boat docks too. And I read that the donor left enough money to hire four times the average number of park rangers compared to the other mainland national parks."

"I loved going to the big valley yesterday and seeing all those buffalo! They are so cute! And I love riding the monorail! Can we ride it again today?" says the older girl while trying to build another layer on her sandcastle. Her little sister keeps burying her own toy.

"We will ride it tomorrow, sweetie. I still can't figure out how they make the monorail go silent and invisible here," the mom says.

"It's the new technology. Maybe the donor invented it?" Jack replies.

"Cookie!" yells the youngest girl, and she stands up, spraying sand from her little legs all over her older sister.

Reese and Dean look at each other quietly. Reese tries to memorize all that the family just said.

"Why did the cookie go to the doctor?" Dean asks, smiling at his older sister.

"Why?" answers Reese, smiling back him and knowing how much he loves his jokes.

"Because it felt crummy!" Dean says with giggles between each word. Reese laughs in response.

Reese motions to Dean to move away from the family. As they stand up, Reese sees a brochure on the ground and picks it up.

# Elf Noises

"What is this place, Reese? Invisible monorails? Buffalo on an island? Biggest national park in our country? Erutuf?" Dean asks in one big breath.

"I guess there's a new national park called Erutuf. Maybe we went to the future in the video? The brochure looks like a real national park brochure, though," Reese says while looking at it.

"Oh, I know! We are in a movie or a book! But I don't want to be in a movie. Maybe a book."

"Maybe? This place sounds really cool! I'm glad you're here with me, though," Reese says as they walk farther toward the water. She puts the brochure into her pocket.

"Maybe we can see buffalo later? Are we invisible to everyone, or just that family there?" Dean asks.

"I doubt that we will see any buffalo here on the beach. I don't know why that family couldn't see or hear us. Strange! Let's go over to the water and then check out this brochure together. It might help explain some things here," Reese replies.

The siblings walk forward and hum a song from the latest animated movie. Reese thinks about how her parents would love this place and wonders when they will see them again. She decides not to say this to Dean because she doesn't want to scare or worry him. She is in charge now and needs to remain calm for him, yet she's not sure how.

"What's that noise?" Dean asks while looking around. They have walked well past where the family once sat. They do not see another person anywhere.

"I didn't hear anything. It was probably just the water or noises out on the ocean," Reese replies while sitting down in the sand.

"It wasn't quiet. It sounded like an elf."

"An elf? You've lost it, brother!" Reese says while drawing a smiley face in the sand with her right hand.

"There! I heard it again!" Dean jumps up and points toward the ocean.

"Okay, I may have heard something. I don't think elves live on this island. Do you?" Reese asks while giving her sand face some long, curly hair.

"Welcome to our home," a voice says.

Both Dean and Reese look at each other. Reese hears it now too.

"Who is there?" Reese asks with a long pause between each word. Dean sits down next to Reese, smashing her sand smiley face. Reese doesn't even notice.

A head pops out from behind them. Dean and Reese look at the little head and then back at each other without saying anything. Dean scoots as close to Reese as possible without sitting on her. Two large eyes stare at them and seem gentle and nice. The eyes sit on a dry, scaly head.

"Well, hello! Welcome!" says the creature. Their eyes move forward over the sand mound, and the large body follows. The flippers rustle in the sand to move closer to Reese and Dean.

"Whoa, it's a talking sea turtle!" Reese exclaims, poking her brother's shoulder right next to her.

"Yes, of course I talk. I was starting to wonder whether you would talk back to me. It's not very nice to not reply hello," says the sea turtle while settling its three-foot-long, three-hundred-pound body near them. The big, gentle eyes stare at them.

"You're the elf?" Dean asks the turtle while rubbing his eyes. Dean does not think that elves should look like turtles.

"I'm not an elf, silly boy. I am a green sea turtle. My name is Emma. Welcome to my home," the turtle says.

"Your name is Emma?" Dean asks, looking at his sister with raised eyebrows.

"She said her name was Emma, Dean. I am Reese, and this is my brother, Dean," Reese says to the turtle, standing up slowly and moving closer to Emma.

"What brings you children to our home? You aren't like the tourists here," Emma says.

"We don't know. We don't even know how we got here, or where we are now. We overheard a family say that we are in Erutuf National Park. Is this right?" Reese asks while squatting down by Emma.

Emma tilts her head and stares at Reese.

"Are there elves here?" Dean asks Emma before she can answer Reese's question.

"No, this isn't the North Pole. Why is he so obsessed with elves?" Emma asks, looking at Reese and shaking her head.

"Dean, are you okay?" Reese asks him without taking her eyes off of Emma.

"Elves seem more real than a talking sea turtle! The turtle is talking, Reese! We are on some unknown island national park, and the turtle is talking!" Dean says, his eyes huge.

"It's okay, Dean. All animals talk," Reese replies.

"Yes, we all talk. Humans aren't the only ones who communicate on this planet," Emma agrees.

"Reese, can we talk alone for a moment?" Dean asks his sister while trying to take a deep breath to slow his heart rate.

"Go on and chat. It's not usual that we get to talk to humans. This might be a bit odd to you," Emma says.

Reese and Dean move a few feet away from Emma and closer to the water. As they stop, Dean hugs his sister hard, almost knocking her over. The ocean water moves to and fro as background noise while the two siblings stand together.

"You okay, Dean?" asks Reese, hugging him back.

"I just think that this is all weird. I'm a little scared. The turtle talks! Why do you think it is totally normal?" Dean replies, letting go of his big hug. He digs his left foot into the sand and watches it cover his toes.

"Hey, I am here with you. Emma seems pretty nice, though. It's pretty cool to see a sea turtle so up close. Maybe she can help us get home? Let's go back and talk to her more. It's a bit weird, but let's figure it out together. I can do the talking if you still feel weird about all of this here."

"Okay, you do the talking," Dean agrees. "I'm going to keep an eye on her. You know, in case she changes into an elf or something. I do like her shell colors and how the brown, green, yellow, and gray mix."

"She's not an elf. I like her shell colors too. Come on," Reese says while taking his hand and walking back to where Emma waited.

"Elf Emma," whispers Dean with a giggle as he goes with Reese. "Reese, what is the first thing that an elf learns in school? The elfabet!" Dean giggles and tugs on Reese's shirt, making her smile.

"Let's get back to Emma, silly," Reese says.

# Tiger Sharks

"Emma, we would like to say we are sorry. We have never seen a turtle talk before other than in the movies. We hope that you understand and aren't mad at us," Reese says to Emma as she sits down next to her.

"And we know that you're not an elf. Sorry," says Dean, sitting next to Reese.

"Thank you. I think that you two might be the ones to help us. But this elf business makes me wonder," says Emma.

"What do you need help with here? It's so beautiful and peaceful here," Reese says.

"Pirates," Emma replies calmly.

"Pirates!" yells Dean.

"Does he like pirates as much as he likes elves?" Emma asks Reese.

"Real pirates?" Dean asks without allowing Reese to answer Emma.

"Yes, silly. We wouldn't need help with toy pirates," Emma says while pushing her flippers deeper into the sand.

"How can we help you with pirates?" Reese asks.

Emma explains, "Erutuf is a special national park. There are different groups of pirates wanting to take it over, and they have tried coming in on this west side of the island. My family of sea turtles has protected the island so far, but it's getting more difficult. We have kept it safe for some time now, but we are getting worried. Our west side would be the easiest side of this park for them to gain entry because they can't climb mountains and don't seem to like the desert."

"Do we get to battle pirates?" Dean asks Emma while moving a little closer to Emma. He feels more comfortable now talking to the turtle, and he's excited about pirates. Dean has pirates all over his bedroom at home. He even has a treasure map on the ceiling that he stares at every night before falling asleep. He keeps asking for a plank off his bed, but his parents haven't agreed to that yet.

"What is a pirate's favorite thing to do in school?" asks Dean.

"Pirates go to school now?" Emma answers.

"No, the answer is arrrrrt!" Dean replies, shifting his weight around and moving his feet.

"Dean was just telling a pirate joke," Reese explains to a confused Emma.

"Okay, thank you. I didn't think that pirates studied much other than maps and attack strategies. Although some of them might have studied," Emma says.

"Help, help, help!" cries something from the water. The squeaky voice sounds like another elf. The waves look calm, and nothing floats on top.

"Oh, no, that's Colton!" Emma says.

"Who's Colton?" Dean asks while watching Emma move toward the water.

"He's one of us—a sea turtle. Not an elf, as I know you're thinking. He needs help. It might be a tiger shark, or something else," Emma says.

"Let's go help," Reese says, following Emma. Dean stands there frozen, watching Emma and Reese head to the ocean water. Reese moves faster on land and gets to the water first.

"I'm not helping with sharks," Dean whispers to himself. He can't believe his sister is just heading toward possible danger. She would never do this type of thing at home.

"Reese, can you help him?" Emma asks, watching Reese head into the ocean.

Reese is ankle deep, pauses for just a second, and turns around. She nods to Emma and moves forward. The water slowly moves up her legs. Within seconds, the deep blue ocean water covers Reese. Reese takes a deep breath before her head goes under the water. She swims a few feet toward the noise of Colton.

As she swims, Reese notices that she can breathe in this water. It's not like at home in a pool, where she holds her breath when underwater. Reese looks down at her legs and gasps. Her legs aren't there anymore—she has a mermaid tail! She kicks her leg, and the tail moves. The tail sparkles blue and green in the water and is prettier than the ones she sees in books. The scales seem to sparkle brighter here. The colors pop brighter here. Reese rubs her eyes and looks again at her legs to see the tail still there.

"Help, help, help!" cries Colton.

Reese ignores the tail now and swims toward the cries. She sees the blunt nose and narrow snout of the shark first. Then she sees the dark vertical stripes on the large body. The large dorsal fin appears in Reese's view. He's huge! The hair on Reese's arms stand up. The shark moves slow and smooth, yet he zips and zags toward Colton, who is ahead of Reese on the left. Colton swims gracefully away, and Reese sees his large carapace (the external shell) facing the tiger shark. The tiger shark follows Colton. Colton cries for help again.

Reese's heart beat quickens. She knows that she has to help Colton because she doesn't want him to get hurt, or worse. She takes a deep breath and tells herself, "You can do this. Just think."

"Help, help, help!" Colton cries.

Reese looks around her in the blue water. She sees a shiny object under her and grabs it without even thinking. Reese launches this object through the water, aimed to the right of the tiger shark. The tiger shark sees it go by and pauses. He stops his zigzag tracking and follows the shiny object reflecting the sun and floating in the opposite direction of Colton.

Colton notices the shark's turn and heads back to shore at top speed, just in case the shark returns to following him. Colton looks back over his shell every few seconds in case the shark comes back to chase him.

Reese exhales her breath and smiles to herself. She did it. She helped save Colton. She saved a sea turtle in the ocean from a shark—while she had a mermaid tail! Reese thinks about how no one will believe her and swims back to the shore, enjoying her tail.

Colton reaches the shallow water and sees Emma standing there, watching and waiting. Dean stands next to Emma, biting his fingernails.

"Are you okay?" Emma asks Colton as he comes out of the water to her.

"I am okay. Your friend saved me!" Colton says to them, smiling.

"How did Reese do that? How did she hold her breath that long?" Dean asks, rubbing his eyes as he sees his sister swimming to them. She is just a few feet behind Colton.

"Well, at least he didn't call you an elf. I'm glad you're okay, Colton. This is Dean, and his sister, Reese, helped you out. They are our friends here and will help us with the pirates. If he mentions elves, just ignore it," Emma says with confidence in her voice.

"I know that you two are not elves," Dean says to Emma.

"Anyway, Colton, what happened out there?" Emma asks, ignoring Dean.

"Your friend distracted the tiger shark so I could get away. I am so thankful to her," Colton replies.

"Reese distracted a shark?" Dean asks, looking from Colton to Emma and back again.

"Yes, I did," Reese says proudly, walking out the ocean with her head held high. She glances down and sees her legs again. She rubs her hands along her legs for a minute. They feel wet and normal.

"Thank you so much for saving my life! We all appreciate your help against that tiger shark," Colton tells Reese.

Reese leans over and hugs him. "I'm so glad that I could help. Emma, did you say that this is a special national park here? What did you mean by that?"

"Did something special happen in the water?" Emma asks, titling her head to the side.

"You answered my question with a question. I think that this is a special national park. Well, they are all special, but this park seems a bit magical," Reese says softly to Emma.

Dean looks from Reese to Emma and back to Reese. He rubs his forehead and tries to focus on what is going on here.

"What happened in the water, Reese?" Emma asks softly.

"My legs turned to a mermaid tail, and I could breathe easily down there without having to come up for air. My tail was so beautiful and much prettier than the ones in movies," Reese says, looking out at the ocean and then down at her legs.

"What? You turned into a mermaid?" Dean yells, throwing his hands into the air.

"Don't yell, little boy, please. Yes, that's what she said. First it was elves, and now you're yelling about mermaids. It's like you've never done or seen this before," Emma replies.

Reese and Dean stare at her both in silence for a long minute.

"Well, I guess that you haven't seen or become a mermaid before, by the way your jaws are lowered and the complete silence. Especially from elf boy here. His jaw might dig in the sand in a minute! Yes, this is a very special national park. Magic exists here. The magic found you two somehow. We now need your help against the pirates to protect this special place."

Dean touches his jaw and then closes it with his hand.

Colton adds, "Yes, Emma, is right. We need your help. You can sleep in our sandcastle tonight to get some rest. Tomorrow, we can fill you in about the pirates. I think that you both have learned a lot and done a lot for today."

"Good idea, Colton. I will see you later. Elf boy and Reese, follow me," Emma says as she moves down the beach. Reese and Dean look at each and follow in silence behind Emma.

"Did you really fight off a tiger shark?" Dean asks his sister.

Reese replies, "Yeah, it was like I transformed into someone brave and strong. It was pretty cool!"

"That is cool! Hey, what does a snowshark do to you?" asks Dean, smiling at Reese and Emma.

"Oh, no," Emma says.

"It gives you frost bites." Dean giggles at his joke, and Emma and Reese giggle at Dean. Colton looks at the three others and shrugs his turtle shoulders.

# Sandcastles

"Emma, did Colton say that we will sleep in a sandcastle? Or did I just hear him wrong?" Reese asks while following Emma.

"Yes, you will need a good night's rest to help with the pirates. The sandcastle is the perfect place for you both tonight."

"Where is it? I don't see anything big enough for us to sleep in," Reese notes.

"Um, Reese, look over to the right. It's huge!" Dean says, pointing ahead and a bit to the right.

"Wow! Emma, it's beautiful!" Reese says with excitement. There is a bit more bounce in her steps.

"Wait till you see the inside. I think that you will both be happy!" Emma replies, smiling.

They approach the massive sandcastle, and Reese and Dean pause to take in its grandness. This castle is not like the sandcastles regular kids build at the beach. This particular sandcastle stands as big and tall as a real castle. It looks like Neuschwanstein Castle in Germany, the castle Walt Disney modeled Disneyland's castle after, but it is all sand! The tallest tower rises about two hundred feet above the ground. The castle itself spreads out over sixty-seven thousand square feet, which is the size of the entire White House! Towers, turrets, and huge walls, all made of sparkling sand, loom over the children.

Dean rubs his forehead on both sides again and wonders how this castle stands so enormous while being made of sand. He looks to the left and right of it. Yes, it is all sand. Dean thinks that his sister is never going to want to leave the castle. She will probably want him to call her Princess Reese tonight. His eyes roll as he shakes his head.

Reese cannot stop smiling and keeps saying "wow" many times. Emma wears a soft smile while watching the children's reactions.

"Reese, a drawbridge is coming down from the castle!" Dean yells, and he starts running to it. "It's made of sand too!" Dean gets to the bridge and cautiously touches it with his hand before stepping on it.

"I could say something about him to you, Reese, but I will pass on this occasion. I guess you children don't see sandcastles very often," Emma says to Reese.

Reese shakes her head in silence and watches her brother walk like an excited snail across the bridge. He pauses every few moments and touches the bridge with both hands to make sure it will hold him, and then he moves forward.

Emma and Reese follow Dean along the drawbridge. Reese turns around for a moment and looks at the ocean waves. She touches her legs again and wonders how she gathered up the courage to fight a shark. Reese smiles and pats her legs one more time as she jogs to catch up to Emma.

Dean waits for them at the front doors. The doors stand at least fifteen feet tall, which is twice the size of a normal door. Dean touches the doors to make sure that it's really still sand. He turns around to Emma and asks, "How is this all sand?"

She replies with a smile, "Welcome to the magic of Erutuf National Park. Open the Sand Dancer Castle doors, please." With that last statement, the large castle doors open slowly, and instrumental music comes from within the castle.

"I like the castle's name!" Reese whispers.

Dean, Reese, and Emma enter into a great hall and entryway. The hall alone could barely fit inside their school's gymnasium. Grand staircases line both sides of the hall and lead up to the second floor. The staircases curve toward the middle to meet at the large landing. The ornate carpets along the staircases contain colorful little butterflies as patterns covering the sand stairs. A smell of fruit mixed with cotton candy washes over them as they take a few more steps into this massive entryway.

Real butterflies fly around the room. One little purple butterfly lands on Reese's shoulder and says hello in a soft, sweet voice. The baby purple butterfly then flies away to join her friends. Reese giggles softly and waves goodbye to the purple butterfly. A larger yellow butterfly flies to Emma and welcomes her to the castle in her soft voice.

"How is this a sandcastle? It is so cool. Are there butterflies all over? Are they real?" Dean asks.

"It is a sandcastle, and this is the butterfly room. The butterflies stay in this room. Yes, the butterflies are real. Each room has a different theme to it. Reese, you can sleep in the sea turtle room. Dean, you can sleep in the panda room. All the bedrooms and the playroom are upstairs," Emma says.

"Cool, I love pandas!" Dean answers. Reese nods her head in silence, still watching butterflies glide around them.

"Come along with me. I will give you a tour of downstairs. This is the great entry area with the butterflies. Next, we will move into the grand ballroom," Emma tells them.

"It's so beautiful in here. Look at all the shades of blue here," Reese says while walking into the grand ballroom.

The grand ballroom is indeed grand. The school gymnasium plus the neighborhood library could fit inside this room.

"Yes, this room is the blue room here. Some rooms are themed with colors, and some are themed with animals representing various parts of this national park island. The colors all need each other to make a rainbow," Emma explains as she comes into the room behind Reese and Dean.

Reese dances around the room to the music. Her smile grows with each dance step. Dean walks over to a large window and looks out. The ocean looks back at him, with its beautiful blue colors matching some of the blues in this room. He thinks to himself how much his parents would like this national park and castle. Dean misses them. He swallows and turns around to see his sister still dancing.

"Let's go see the other rooms. Next, we have the greeting room. This room is themed green. People come to this room to greet and chat with each other here. You can chat anywhere, but this room is more formal. You can even have tea service in here," Emma shares with Reese and Dean.

"Let's chat, sister. Formal chat," Dean says, and he lies down on the emerald green sofa.

"You're so silly. These greens are so pretty here. I love it all. Someday, I want an emerald ring like that sofa color. I bet the tea cups are green here too!" Reese comes over and pets the super soft green sofa after moving Dean's feet off it. Pale green curtains line the windows. The floor has grass-like soft carpet. A real evergreen tree stands tall in a corner, seemingly guarding the room.

"What is the next room? This castle is amazing!" Reese says while heading to the next door. Dean hops off the sofa and joins Emma and his sister.

"Yeep! Wow! Just wow! I'm not leaving here," Dean yells when he enters the next room.

"I think you could name this room and color here, elf boy," Emma says, smiling at Dean. Dean does not even hear her name for him—all he can see are books everywhere.

"I've never seen a library like this one. Dean may seriously never leave here. I love this ruby red color," Reese says.

The room has at least four stories to it, and at least fifty rows of books line the walls. Two spiral staircases await someone to climb them to reach the high rows of books. A globe the size of small car sits by a window. Four wooden desks with comfy red chairs scatter the room. A ruby red carpet covers the floor, and matching red curtains line the windows.

"Look up on the ceiling, Dean," Reese suggests to her brother. Dean glances up and gasps. The ceiling contains a number of famous book quotes written in the same ruby red.

"I think that this library has about every book. So, anything you want should be in here," Emma tells them.

"I cannot believe that you have this many books in a sandcastle! There are mountains and loads and heaps of books here!" Dean says as he walks up to a wall of books. He reaches out his arms and hugs the wall.

"Elf boy is quite unique, Reese," Emma whispers to her.

"He really loves to read. I think this room might be better than anything he ever imagined. Thank you for sharing this castle with us. It is quite magical here. We love it!" Reese replies. Emma nods back to her.

"Maybe those boys wouldn't make fun of me reading if they saw a library like this one?" Dean says aloud.

"The boys at school aren't nice. Don't think about those bullies now, Dean. Enjoy this room!" Reese tells him. A couple of classmates have teased Dean about the amount of time and the number of books he reads. His parents and teacher tell him to ignore their comments, but it can be tough when other kids laugh with the mean boys. It feels like the whole class is laughing at him.

"Let's move on to the rest of the tour. After I'm done, you both can explore the castle on your own," Emma suggests, and she moves to the next room. Reese follows, and Dean reluctantly leaves the library. He glances back at all the books and smiles at them.

"The next room is pretty much what it looks like: a dining room. This is our purple room. The kitchen is next and is the orange room. Yes, we always have lots of oranges in there to eat. I hope you like oranges. Feel free to eat anything in there," Emma explains as Reese and Dean follow her around this enormous first floor.

"I will let you both explore upstairs on your own because I need to get back to the other turtles. You will find the rainbow playroom and bedrooms with animal themes like pandas, sea turtles—my favorite, of course—polar bears, bison, cheetahs, and a few others. We have bathrooms throughout both levels, and you can use any of them. As a reminder, Reese, you will sleep in the sea turtle room and Dean will be in the panda room. I will come back here first thing in the morning after breakfast so we can get ready for the pirates. I hope you both enjoy the castle and sleep well!" Emma says.

Dean lunges forward and wraps his arms around Emma in a big hug.

"Okay, elf boy, thanks for the hug," Emma says, scooting backward from Dean and his arms. Dean rubs the top of Emma's head before she scoots too far away.

"Thank you, Emma. We will take good care of the castle," Reese says while her eyes examine every inch of the room.

Emma leaves through the large front doors.

# Panda Help

"**R**ace you upstairs!" Dean says, and he takes off running up the sand stairs. Reese follows a few stairs behind him and almost catches him, but Dean beats her. Reese stops at the top of the stairs to catch her breath.

"Let's go to the right and see what's over here," Reese says between deep breaths after running and trying to catch her speedy brother.

Reese and Dean walk into the playroom. Emma was not joking about it being a rainbow theme. The tall walls have millions of rainbows painted all over them. Some rainbows tilt to the right and some tilt to the left. Some rainbows even sit upside down.

Toys line the rainbow-colored storage containers containing Legos, dolls, balls, video games, action figures, board games, and many other toys. More toys fill this room than the toy aisles at Target!

At the far end of the room, a rainbow crafting table sits with lots of paper, markers, crayons, and a kit with other crafting tools. A rainbow dollhouse guards the side wall.

"I cannot believe this castle!" Reese says to Dean as he picks up a toy basketball and shoots it into a basket.

"What do you think Emma needs us to do with the pirates? I hope we get to battle them. I have been practicing for years!" Dean says.

"I don't know. They are probably not real pirates or the scary kind, Dean. And practicing pirate battles with your little friends won't be the same."

"Well, I am ready, and I think that they will be real. The turtles need help, so they must be real. This castle is so cool! Let's go check out our rooms," Dean says while dribbling another ball. Reese follows him out of the room carrying a rainbow pinwheel that she blows on to make it spin.

"Pandas!" Dean yells from the second bedroom down the hall. Reese enters his room and sees pandas everywhere. There is a giant panda bed with stuffed panda toys on it. The desk looks like a bamboo tree with a panda chair. The wallpaper is covered with pandas playing around in a bamboo forest. The soft green carpet tickles their toes.

"Did you see that on the wall over there, Reese?" Dean asks, pointing to the wall near a window.

"See what? I see lots of pandas in here!"

"The panda on the wall moved," Dean says while touching the wallpaper. It feels like a normal wall and regular wallpaper.

"You just want them to move and be alive like the butterflies. They can't have real pandas in here. Can you imagine the bison room? One would barely fit in there!"

"No, it moved. I swear that a panda was sitting here by this piece of bamboo on the wall, and it stood up and moved away. It ran too fast, though," Dean replies.

"You're seeing things. I'm going to go see my room!"

"Okay, I'm going to stay here a few minutes and see if this panda moves again."

"You're so silly," Reese says as she heads to the next bedroom.

Reese opens the door, and the smell of the ocean air engulfs her. She breathes it in. Somehow a cool breeze goes throughout the room. Sand tickles her toes instead of carpet or hardwood floors. Deep blue water color paints the walls. Sea turtles decorate the walls in various sizes of paintings. A large sea turtle painting sits above the large canopy bed.

Reese jumps onto the bed and snuggles up to a stuffed sea turtle toy. She thinks that Emma must love this room!

"Reese, it moved again!" Dean shouts from his bedroom. Reese runs into the room still holding her stuffed sea turtle, whom she named Emma.

"Look, the panda was in this spot when you left. Now he is over here," Dean says, pointing about a foot away from the original spot.

"It did move. This castle is so cool! It's like he's playing hide-and-seek with you. I wonder if something magical happens in each room?" Reese replies, squeezing her new stuffed animal tighter.

"This place is so cool! I don't want to go to bed. Can we stay up late tonight?" Dean asks, putting his hands together in a pleading position.

"I guess so. There's no one here to tell us to go bed! I think it's just me and you here. Emma said she would be back in the morning."

"So cool! Preston will never believe this story when I tell him back in school. He would love that cheetah room down the hall. He runs fast, but I am still the fastest kid in second grade," Dean tells his sister. He wishes his best friend, Preston, could be here too. Preston just moved to their area about a year ago, but Dean and Preston quickly became best friends.

"I wish Olivia was here too! She loves butterflies so much and might not leave that room!" Reese says. Reese met Olivia on the first day of kindergarten, and they have been best friends since. They play on the same soccer team and love animals. "Come see my room."

Dean agrees and follows Reese to her sea turtle room. They sit together on the large bed and look around the room. They both wait to see what might happen magical in this room. A few minutes of quiet go by.

"Why don't fish play basketball? They're afraid of nets!" says Dean, breaking the silence in the sea turtle room as he giggles.

"Hmph. I bet sea turtles don't like nets either," Reese replies.

"You're like Emma now. That was a joke. Get it— basketball nets?"

"I get it. I was just thinking about nets and turtles getting caught in them," Reese says while staring at one colorful sea turtle painting on the wall. She takes a deep breath in and out.

"Are you okay, Reese?"

"Yes, I guess I am just tired. I might go to sleep. You can stay up if you want."

"I'm not tired yet. Can we have a sleepover in here?" Dean asks.

"You don't want to sleep in your own room?" Reese replies, raising her right eyebrow.

"Maybe. Tonight we can sleep in this room, and tomorrow we can sleep in my panda room. I want to stay with you. I don't want to be alone."

"I understand. It will be fun to be together. I'm going to get ready for bed. They even have some sea turtle pajamas over here on the table." Reese says while getting off the bed and heading to the table.

"Oh, I'll go and see if I have panda ones in my room. I'm also going to go grab a book from the library. I'll meet you back here."

Dean goes back into his panda room. He looks at the dresser and spots a shirt and pair of shorts panda pajamas. As he changes into the new pajamas, he sees the panda on the wallpaper move again. This time the panda waves at him. Dean closes his eyes and shakes his head. When he opens his eyes, the panda is still waving to him. Dean moves closer to the panda. The panda trots along the wallpaper to a new location.

"What is this little panda doing?" Dean says to himself. Dean follows the panda around the room until the panda stops. The panda points to something, and Dean looks at it. "What is that, panda buddy?" Dean asks him. The panda points harder at it. Dean squats down and looks at the panda. The panda's eyes grow big as Dean stares back at him. The panda nods his soft black and white head and points again.

"Is this what you want me to see, panda buddy?" Dean sees an $X$ on the wallpaper. He stands up tall and nods to the panda. "Reese, come down here," he calls to his sister. The panda nods again. The panda then shivers while staring at the X. "Okay, he wants us to see the X. I wonder why, though? Maybe Reese will know."

"What's up? Wait till you see the rainbow toothpaste that they have here! It is so cool!" Reese says after coming into the panda room.

"Reese, the panda moved again. This time he waved me to follow him and stopped at this X on the wall."

Reese looks at the wall and at the panda. The panda looks right into Reese's eyes and nods. Reese jumps back a bit. "He is alive on there!" Reese yells. She slowly moves forward again.

"Duh, Reese, this castle has lots of alive and weird things here. He wants us to know about the X. What do you think the X is?"

"I still can't believe the wallpaper is telling us something," Reese says.

"Oh, but talking turtles are okay? Seriously?" Dean asks.

"Okay, okay. So he's pointing to an X here. Hmm." Reese thinks a few minutes. "Maybe the X has to do with the pirates. Pirates seem to like Xs." At this comment, the wallpaper panda jumps up and down. He gives Dean and Reese and a big smile. The panda then shivers again.

"Oh, I wish I could hug him," Dean says, smiling as big as the wallpaper panda.

"You want to hug wallpaper?"

"You know what I mean!"

"Are you cold, little panda?" Reese asks, noticing the panda shivering. He shakes his head and points to the X.

"I think he's trying to tell us one more thing about the X," Dean notes. The panda nods and shivers again.

"Are the pirates somewhere where it is cold on this island?" Reese asks. The panda shakes his head.

"Are you scared, panda buddy?" Dean asks. The panda nods.

"Are you scared of the pirates here?" Reese asks him. The panda nods again.

"Are you trying to tell us to be careful with them?" Dean asks. The panda nods yet again. Dean smiles and says, "Thank you, panda buddy, but we will be okay!"

"That's so sweet of you, panda. We will be extra careful! We appreciate your help," Reese adds. The panda nods and smiles big at both of them. "Okay, so we need to do something with the X with the pirates tomorrow and be careful. I think that we should go to bed now and rest up for tomorrow."

"Yep! I am kind of tired. Thank you, panda buddy! We will take care of it, so don't be scared or worry anymore," Dean tells the panda. The wallpaper panda gives Dean a thumbs-up in return. Dean smiles back and chases after his sister, who has already left the room.

# The Mission

The bright sun blasts into the sea turtle room and wakes up Reese and Dean. Both kids slept hard after all the excitement of the national park island yesterday.

Reese jumps out of bed and gets dressed in the time it takes Dean to yawn. Dean moves out of bed like he has all day to do it. Reese looks at the sea turtle paintings on the wall and smiles.

"I love this room! Come on, Dean. We need to eat some breakfast before Emma gets here. She said that she'd be here early."

"Okay, okay. I'm still tired."

"You can nap later. Let's go!" Reese says, tugging him to his clothes on the floor. "I'll meet you in the kitchen."

Dean finally comes downstairs to the kitchen. The orange kitchen smells like a diner on a Saturday morning full of breakfast smells. Reese delivers two plates to the table with pancakes, bacon, and some fresh orange juice.

"When did you learn to cook?" Dean asks her while taking a huge first bite.

"Uncle Neal taught me during their last visit to our house," Reese says before taking her first bite.

"I didn't know that he taught you how to cook breakfast. This is all really good! Thanks!" Dean is hard to understand with food in his mouth. Reese smiles back at him, feeling proud. Her mom never lets her do important things at home, and it feels great to do something significant like make breakfast.

"Good morning," squeaks a tiny voice from below them.

"Now, that's an elf! I bet we missed the elf room here," Dean says between bites.

"Miss Emma said that the boy might think that I am an elf. I'm down here—and not an elf. My name is Ava," squeaks the voice.

"Oh, you are so adorable! Dean, she is a baby sea turtle. Good morning, Ava," Reese says. She walks over to Ava and squats down to talk to her. At birth, sea turtles are only about two inches long. Ava is about this size.

"Miss Emma gave me one big job before heading out the ocean for my first time. My job is to take you to Miss

Emma for your day. Most of the time, we babies have to go straight to the water, but Miss Emma made an exception for me today. I am very proud," Ava squeaks.

"Are elves related to sea turtles somehow?" Dean asks Reese while munching a piece of crispy bacon.

"No, you dummy. Let's get going with Ava," Reese whispers. Then she turns to Ava and says, "You're doing great at your job and should be proud!"

"Thank you. Follow me," Ava says and she heads slowly down the hall and out of the castle.

Dean grabs his orange juice and chugs the last few sips from it. He places the cup down and takes one more piece of bacon for the walk. Reese and Dean follow along behind Ava as she leaves the orange kitchen.

"I want fresh oranges in my kitchen when I'm a grown-up. I like that type of kitchen," Reese says.

"I can't wait to see the ocean home for me," Ava chimes in to Reese and Dean.

"Well, I want a talking panda room and a huge library in my future house," Dean says. Ava smiles. Reese thinks about the sandcastle as they walk along, and she wonders what will happen next on this amazing island here.

"What is a pirate's favorite letter?" Dean asks his sister.

"That one is easy: *Y*."

"Nope, *Rrr*," Dean replies, and he giggles.

Ava, Reese, and Dean arrive at the same part of the beach as yesterday. Emma turns around as they come up to her.

"Good morning, all. Thank you so much, Ava. I am very proud of you. You will do well. You may head out to the water now," Emma says with a nod to Ava.

"Thank you, Miss Emma. Good luck to you both," Ava replies, and she makes her way to the calm ocean in front of them.

"Bye, Ava. Thank you for the escort here to the beach. We liked walking with you," Reese says.

"Well, did you both enjoy your stay at our castle?" Emma asks.

"It was magical! Thanks!" Reese replies.

"Why did the panda show us an *X*?" Dean asks Emma before Reese could finish.

"Elf boy, you are unique. Humans need to learn politeness. I asked you how the night went."

"I'm sorry, Emma. It was really cool. I love the castle. The moving panda on the wall was really fun," Dean replies while looking down at his feet. Dean feels like a schoolteacher has just reprimanded him for shouting out the answer, and it doesn't feel good. Dean wishes that he didn't have to feel that way here on this cool national park island, but there are teacher types everywhere.

"Thank you for your apology. I know that apologizing is not always easy. So, you want to know about the *X* and the panda?" Emma replies, shifting her large body closer to Dean.

"Yes. I think that it has something to do with the pirates."

"We both think that it has something to do with pirates," Reese agrees.

"Well, you are smart children. You are correct," Emma says. Dean dabs by dropping his head into the bent crook of a slanted, upwardly angled arm, while raising the opposite arm out straight in a parallel direction. Then he looks up at Emma and smiles.

"Strange moves indeed. Anyway, about the X that you saw in the castle and the pirates," Emma continues, trying to hide her amusement at Dean. Reese and Dean scoot closer to Emma and await her next words with complete attention. Reese kneels in the sand. Dean leans on his left side like he is posing for a magazine or photo shoot.

"I mentioned a bit about it yesterday, but I will share more with you now. For years, pirates have tried to come here and find these secret maps. Pirates from many organizations have tried. The pirate groups look different and have different leaders. Some pirates operate on their own. They all want the maps here," Emma explains.

"What maps? The ones in the panda room? I didn't see a full map on the wall there. We only saw the X." Dean asks.

"No, the panda was trying to ask you to help us with these maps," Emma replies.

"How can we help? We are just kids. I don't understand," Reese says. She frowns in frustration at Emma.

"As you both know now, this is a different type of national park. It is a very large island with magical abilities. The abilities here vary based on the area and the animals in that part of the island. You have seen the sea turtles' magic along the beaches."

"Yes, this is a cool national park island. What do the maps have on them that is so special to these pirates?" Reese asks, shifting from sitting on her knees to crisscross.

"Do the pirates have tattoos and carry swords? We need some swords to battle with them. Do you have some here for us?" Dean asks.

"The pirates look and act different. It depends which group comes. For example, one pirate group looks like businessmen at a corporate meeting, with them all dressed in three piece-suits and ties. I think that group carries handguns as their weapon of choice," Emma explains.

"Suits? What kind of goofy group of pirates wears suits? They need to wear bandanas and torn pants and go barefoot," Dean says.

"Each group is different. This isn't the 1900s, and this isn't *Pirates of the Caribbean*. Clothing varies among the pirates like it varies among you kids today."

"Weird," Dean says.

"We saw another group of pirates that looked like surfer dudes. They got distracted pretty easily with our great surfing waters up the coast. I think someone hired those guys because they didn't seem to care much about their mission after finding some cool waves."

"So how do you know if they are pirates or just tourists here, if they don't dress like pirates?" Reese asks.

"We know for a few reasons. We have seen these pirates for many, many years. Tourists usually just do touristy activities: they hike, look at animals, and try to relax. These pirates have a specific mission or destination. The pirates also don't care about the animals. Most people at a national park care about the animals. For example, the pirates came in here during baby turtle hatch time and blocked the path to the ocean for a number of the babies. The pirates were trying to get what they thought was a map." Emma explains to Dean and Reese.

"Oh, those poor little babies." Reese replies with a large frown.

"We will protect all babies on our mission!" Dean adds.

"These pirates are not like the ones that you think about or have seen in the movies. They do not care about others and only want to accomplish their mission. I need to warn you that there is danger involved in helping us, but I think that you both can handle it. Even you, elf boy," Emma says.

"Oh, we can easily deal with pirates and any type of pirate! Count on us, Emma!" Dean says, and he stands to salute Emma.

"What are you doing, elf boy? This isn't the army. Reese, are you sure you two are related? Can he handle this assignment?" Emma asks.

"He's just excited. He can handle it. And we are willing to help! What is next?" Reese says.

"Do we protect the map and battle whoever shows up?" Dean asks quickly.

"No. I will tell you what is next for you both."

"Can I ask a quick question?" Reese asks.

"Yes, go ahead."

"After we help with the pirates, will you or someone else here be able to help us get back home? We really like this place and you, but we miss our parents and Tutu!" Reese says in a quiet voice. She looks over at Dean. She really misses her parents and dog, but she tries to hide it from Dean. She doesn't want to upset him.

"Reese, I understand. Yes, we can help you return home after your assignment. Why do you miss a tutu? Are you missing dance classes?" Emma replies.

"No, Tutu isn't a ballet tutu. Tutu is our dog. She's part of our family, and I miss her." Reese giggles at the thought of her big dog wearing a ballet tutu.

"Do we get to fly through the website again to go home? That was crazy cool," Dean says.

"Interesting dog name. You will see later on about how you will return home. Any other questions before we talk about your assignment?" Emma asks.

"I don't have any other questions, but I would like to thank you for taking such good care of us. Our parents would love you!" Reese says.

Emma nods, and blushes a bit, with some pink coming to her face. "Okay, now back to your assignment."

"Can we call it a mission? Missions sounds way cooler," Dean interrupts.

"Sure, elf boy. If it makes you happy, we will call it your mission. Let me guess: you like spies as much as you like pirates."

"Nope, pirates beat out spies. But spies are cool," Dean replies.

"Okay, your mission is pretty straightforward. You both need to find the sea turtle map somewhere on the beach part of this island. Once you find the map, you need to hide it somewhere new. We have kept the pirates confused by relocating the special map every few years," Emma explains.

"Emma, why don't you or another turtle relocate the map?" Reese asks.

"We do not want to know the location of the map or have any knowledge of where it is located. Therefore, please do not tell me after you finish your mission."

"Why?" Dean asks.

"The pirates have tried to make us tell them where they could find the map in the past. These tactics do not work on us because we do not know."

"Oh, that's pretty cool. We get to do a secret mission!" Dean says, nodding his head at Reese.

"Oh, and there's one more part of the mission. If you encounter pirates, defend the map at all costs. You may even have to battle them," Emma says.

Dean pumps his fist into the air. "Oh, I knew that we would get to battle them. Yes!"

"Don't worry about anything, Emma. We can handle this mission," Reese says.

"Thank you both. I will return to the ocean now. But I will come out here when you return after completing the mission. I wish you both the best. And we sea turtles appreciate your help. Goodbye, and good luck!"

"Bye, Emma. See you soon!" Reese says. Dean echoes her goodbye.

# The Map

Reese and Dean watch Emma head to the ocean water. After she enters the water, Dean jumps up and down and yells, "Yahoo, we have a mission! And we get to see pirates!"

"Really?" Reese asks. She pulls him down from a midair jump. "We need to talk about our first move here. Where should we look for the map?"

"Hey, Reese, what is on the map? Emma never told us."

"I don't know. I guess we will see whatever is on it when we find it."

"What if it is a trail to a million dollars?" Dean asks with a huge grin.

"Seriously, I don't think that it leads to money," Reese replies, rolling her eyes at her brother.

"It could be! What do pirates usually want? Money or gold! That's it—the map must lead to gold. We get to find a map to find gold. So cool! Preston will never believe this adventure—that I get to find a map, find some gold, and maybe battle pirates."

"Well, whatever the map leads to, it must be pretty important to Emma and this national park, so I don't think that it's gold or money. You do realize that if it leads to money or gold, we don't get any of it. Our mission is to find the map and relocate it. We aren't supposed to follow the map," Reese replies.

"You're no fun. We could add that step in there. Please? How often will we ever get to hold a real treasure map and not see where it goes? What are they hiding here that all these pirates want?" Dean asks.

"I don't know. But we told Emma that we would do the mission."

"We are doing the mission. Just adding some fun to it! Please?"

"Well, we can't even follow the map until we find it. We can talk about that after we find the map. Should we search the beach here and head south first?" Reese says, knowing that she will not follow the map or look for the gold. However, she needs to get Dean focused so they can find the map.

"Sounds good to me. Let's go find a map!" Dean says, and he skips down the beach a few feet.

Reese and Dean walk together along the beach in silence. Dean stops and starts digging in the sand.

"What are you doing, Dean?"

"Looking for a map. It could be buried in the sand."

"It seems kind of crazy to bury it here in the sand. I don't know. It seems like a waste of time to do that. Let's keep walking," Reese replies. Dean stands up and follows his older sister.

After another thirty minutes of walking down the beach, Dean plops down on the sand. He lands hard and grunts, and then he shuffles some sand around his feet. His expression looks like when someone takes away one of his books.

"Dean, what's wrong?"

"What are we doing? I'm tired of just walking. When will we find the map?" Dean asks, rubbing his eyes.

"Let's rest here. What about if we go check out the tree area, where we saw that family when we first got to the island?" Reese suggests.

"Okay, fine. I'm not happy right now," Dean replies, kicking some sand around her feet.

"Well, what if I tell you a joke?" Reese asks, hoping this question will cheer him up and motivate him to keep going.

"What? You don't know any jokes!" Dean shoots back.

"Yes, I do! You aren't the only funny one in our family." Reese puts her hands on her hips.

"Yes, I am, and I can easily outjoke you!" Dean says, jumping up and starting to walk with Reese.

"What does outjoke even mean?" Reese asks as they continue toward the tree from yesterday.

"Duh, it means tell the better joke!" Dean replies. He wonders how his sister doesn't know this word.

"Fine. Tell me a joke, and then I will tell you mine," Reese suggests, smiling.

"Why are you smiling? I am about to outjoke you!"

"No way, brother! I am going to do the outjoking today!"

"You didn't know what the word meant until a few minutes ago. No way back!"

"I can still beat you!" Reese says. She walks faster, excited about the possibility of beating her brother at a joke. She also sees the tree not far away.

"You go first, jokester sister!" Dean says.

"Okay, give me a minute to think of my best one."

"You need more than a minute," Dean taunts. He giggles.

"Why did the leaf go to the doctor?" Reese asks.

"Why?"

"Because it was feeling green." Reese giggles now.

"Not bad. Here's mine now. What kind of shorts do clouds wear? Thunderwear!" Dean says giggling hard, and

Reese joins in. The two siblings collide while walking together and laughing out loud.

"I think that you win. Your joke was great!" Reese says between laughs.

"I knew that I would remain king of the jokes in our family! But I'll admit that your joke was better than I thought that it would be," Dean replies.

"Here's the tree from yesterday. You look over by that area, and I will look over by this area. No one is around today, so that is good. And no signs of pirates here," Reese notes.

"I'm on it. I want to find this map! Seeing pirates would be cool too, though," Dean replies.

Reese and Dean spend at least an hour looking under leaves, in the sand, and by the tree. They don't see a map anywhere. Dean and Reese keep searching, although they are moving a little slower with the passing minutes.

"I don't think that the map is here, and I'm hungry." Dean says, breaking the silence and sitting down under the tree in the shade.

"You're always hungry! I don't think the map is here either. We have looked everywhere around this tree area. Where else do you think it could be? We haven't tried the north side of the beach," Reese says as she sits down next to him.

"I don't think that it would be on the beach. What if the tide changes too fast and takes it out to the ocean? The only indoor place that I can think of is the sandcastle."

"That's it—the sandcastle! You're so smart! Let's go!" Reese replies.

"You think that it could be inside there somewhere?" Dean asks.

"Why not the castle?" Reese says with a grin. She stands up and shakes the sand from her legs.

"Okay, let's go. We can eat there too!" Dean says. He stands up to follow her and rubs his tummy in his excitement for some food.

Reese and Dean walk back along the beach to the sandcastle. As they walk along, they talk about the castle and their favorite rooms. Reese and Dean both look forward to having another reason to check out the huge castle again. Dean forgets his hunger in all the excitement of going back to the castle.

"Where does Superman go to shop?" Dean asks while walking.

"Target!" Reese answers.

"No, that would be Captain America. Superman goes to the supermarket," Dean says with a few giggles.

Reese rolls her eyes at this particular joke. "I like Captain America better anyway. And Mom definitely likes going to Target more than the supermarket."

"True. It's still a funny joke," Dean says with a big smile.

"Hey, what's the sparkly thing over there by the drawbridge to the castle?" Reese asks. She doesn't wait for an answer and takes off running. Dean picks up his pace and follows her to the sparkle.

Reese squats down low to the sand. She picks up the little sparkly, shiny object with great care.

"What is it?" Dean asks, looking over her shoulder at the little object in her hand.

"I don't know. It looks like a coin of some kind. It has a castle on this side," Reese replies. She flips over the circular object.

"What's the other side of it?" Dean asks.

"It looks like a bison. I wonder if this has something to do with the map or pirates? Do you think that the castle on here is this sandcastle?" Reese flips it over again to the front.

"Maybe. Can I hold it?"

"Sure, but be careful," Reese replies.

"Why? Will the coin bite me?" Dean asks.

"Just be careful," Reese says as she hands the coin over to Dean. "We might need this coin for something."

Dean holds the coin and then rubs both sides of it. Nothing happens. He hands the coin back to his sister. Reese takes the coin and places it into her pocket.

"Let's keep going and head into the castle now," Reese says. Dean nods and follows along.

# The Coin

Reese and Dean walk on the drawbridge and into the castle. They pause at the door.

"What did Emma say when we entered the castle last time?" Dean asks.

"I think she said something like, 'Welcome to the magic of Erutuf National Park. Open the Sand Dancer Castle doors, please.'" The large castle doors open slowly, and instrumental music comes from within the castle just like the first time.

Butterflies greet Reese and Dean, fluttering around the great hall and entryway. One butterfly lands on Reese's shoulder, and she giggles. Another butterfly seems to dance in front of Dean's nose. He tries to move away, and it follows him for a few minutes.

"This is such a cool way to come into a house or castle," Reese says.

"It is! Hey, let's go ask the panda in my room where to look," Dean suggests, and he heads up the stairs without waiting for an answer.

"Wait for me. He might be able to help us," Reese replies. She takes every other step up the stairs.

Dean and Reese enter the panda bedroom. Dean walks over to where he last saw the moving panda on the wall. He pauses and looks around the room. None of the pandas move. Reese joins him and also examines the wall. They each take two walls to search for the moving panda. Neither one can find a moving panda.

"Hello, panda buddy? We are back and could use some help. Wave to us if you can hear me," Dean says. Dean and Reese stay still and look around.

"I don't see anything moving, Dean. I think that we should start looking around the castle room by room," Reese suggests.

"No way. Do you remember how huge this castle is here? It would take us days to find anything in here. We don't even know how big or little this map is, or its colors. There has to be another clue," Dean says. He sits down on the panda bed.

"Do you think that the coin is a clue?" Reese pulls it out of her pocket.

"Maybe. It does seem funny that it popped up out of nowhere when we are looking for a map. And it does have the castle on the one side," Dean replies. He leans over to Reese and examines the coin over her shoulder. "Wait a minute. Isn't there a bison bedroom in this castle, on this floor?"

"Yes, I think so. Let's go check it out!" Reese says. They scurry out of the panda room. As they leave this room, the panda buddy smiles and waves to them without them noticing him.

Dean and Reese enter the bison bedroom, which is five rooms down from the sea turtle bedroom. As they enter, the room smells like the dust from the Wild West. Air in the room whips around. Dean looks around for tumbleweeds. On the far wall, a huge bison stands tall, taking up the entire wall. He moves his feet to kick up some dust and grunts.

"Ah, Dean, he won't charge at us, will he?" Reese asks as she moves back a couple of feet. She looks around at the other walls. Those walls have professional photographs of bison on them. None of them move or grunt.

"Nah, I bet he's nice. Hi, bison buddy," Dean says.

The bison looks over at Dean and grunts again.

"Okay, let's make this a quick search in this bedroom. Let's look for the map and give the big guy some space," Reese suggests. She starts looking through the drawers in the dresser. Dean moves over to the bed decorated with ropes around it. The bison grunts again as they continue to search for the map.

"It has to be in here," Dean says to himself while looking under the bed.

"Don't give up yet! Once we find it, we can grab some food in the kitchen and talk about where we should we hide it next. Think food!" Reese says. She closes the bottom drawer of the dresser. The bison grunts again.

"I'm going to check under the pillow next, Reese."

"What do you think, that the tooth fairy put it there? I'll check the closet."

"Ha-ha, you're funny. I bet that I find the map first."

"No way. I have much better finding skills than you."

"Says who?" Dean asks.

"Says me." Reese opens the closet doors. The bison on the wall grunts loudly this time. Dean and Reese pause and look at each other. A loud banging noise comes from downstairs.

"Reese, what is that noise?" Dean asks. He moves over to her by the closet doors. The bison grunts loud again.

"I don't know. Let's both go in the closet for a minute, just to be safe." Reese doesn't wait for a response and grabs Dean's arm as he stands frozen by the door. She drags him into the closet and closes the door. They both crouch down on the floor of the dark closet and wait. Neither one speaks. The bison also goes quiet and no longer grunts.

Reese and Dean hear loud footsteps pounding the stairs and then coming down the hall. Dean grabs his sister's hand. She gives him a soft squeeze as she continues to hold his hand. They both sit in the closet without making a noise.

Dean's body shakes, and he scoots as close to Reese without sitting on her.

The door creaks open to this bison bedroom. Dean and Reese hold their breath. Footsteps pound into the room. The heavy steps move around the room for a few minutes that feel like hours. The door to their room closes, and the steps move down the hallway. Then the noises stop. Reese and Dean finally exhale their breaths. The bison lets out a quiet, small grunt.

"I think that person is gone now. The bison seems to be telling us to come out," Dean whispers.

"I don't know. I think that we should wait a few more minutes. What if he hears us move and comes back in here?" Reese whispers back. Dean and Reese remain still in the closet.

After a few minutes, Dean stands up and stretches his arms up into the air. Reese stands next to him. She opens the closet door just a bit and peeks into the room. The bison grunts. She opens the door with caution and steps softly back into the room. Dean follows behind her.

"Do you think that was a pirate?" Dean asks.

"It would make sense. Who else would be in this castle?" Reese answers.

"He had really loud footsteps. Or he was just really big," Dean notes. Reese nods in agreement. "Although I want to see a real pirate, I don't want a big one." Dean states.

"I really don't want to see any pirates. Let's just find the map. It has to be in here, right?" Reese says. The bison grunts again. Reese and Dean look at the bison together.

"He's helping us! Thanks, bison buddy," Dean says. He walks over to the bed and pulls up the sheets, but he doesn't see a map or anything. He lifts one of the pillows up. A small scroll of paper sits there. The bison grunts three times.

"Reese, I found it! I can't believe it! Here is the map!" Dean says.

"What? Under the pillow?" Reese replies. She runs over to the side of the bed. Dean's smile covers his entire face. He lifts the scroll of paper with extreme caution.

"Can we open it and look at it?" Dean asks his sister.

"I guess so. Emma didn't tell us not to open it. I am a little curious about it." Reese shrugs her shoulders. The bison grunts again.

"Bison buddy agrees that we should open it! I'll do it," Dean says, still smiling. He pulls slightly on the twine around the scroll.

Dean unrolls the scroll slowly. Reese starts bouncing up and down while waiting for him, but she doesn't want to hurry him and cause him to rip it. Dean lays out the map on the bison bed, and the two hover over the map for a few minutes in silence.

Dean finally breaks the silence and asks Reese, "What is all of it? Is it even this island?"

"I have no idea. It looks like it leads to a key. There's a key symbol instead of an $X$ marking something. Unless the key is just an $X$ and not a real key," Reese replies, still staring at the map. The map keeps trying to curl back closed, so Dean holds on to two opposite corners. Dean grunts like the bison while trying to keep the map flat. The bison on the wall grunts back. Reese jumps at the grunts and looks around the room.

"We should hide it fast. What if that big pirate guy comes back in here?" Reese suggests.

"We just got the map, and you already want to hide? We should check it out a little bit. That big guy is gone."

"I don't know, Dean. I don't like holding on to the map too long. We need to help Emma and all her friends."

"We will. Let's just keep it for a few more hours. What could go wrong?" Dean says.

"Okay, just a few hours. Then we hide it. Deal?"

"Deal!" Dean replies.

"Okay, so this goofy map. What do you think it is?" Reese asks. She looks back at the map and holds down another corner.

"I remember reading a book where the author coded the map for the main character to find the treasure. Maybe this map is coded, or symbolic, or flipped around somehow."

"How do we know if it's coded, or just not a real map?" Reese asks.

"We know it's not a real version of this island, right? We saw the brochure of this national park back when we saw the family. Actually, do you still have that map?"

"I think so. Let me check my bag." Reese opens up her little bag, digs around, and finds the national park brochure. She pulls it out while trying to not lose other items in her bag. Reese lays the national park brochure map next to the new map. "Look at the shapes of the islands. They're the same. So this scrolled map is this island! It just looks so different."

"Well, we haven't seen much of the island yet," Dean replies.

"I know. The maps just look so different compared to each other."

"It must be a code or something about this island. What could it be to make it look different yet the same island shape?" Dean thinks aloud while staring hard at the map. He rubs his eyes and then focuses.

Reese lets him think for a few minutes. She knows that he has read a lot of books and loves maps. Reese just sees two maps with the same island on them, but they do seem different. She is confident Dean will figure this out.

"I don't know. I love maps, but this thing seems weird," Dean finally says.

"Keep trying. You can get it!" Reese encourages him. She worries if he can't get it, he will be so disappointed. Dean gets really hard on himself when he can't solve a puzzle. He spent weeks trying to solve a Rubik's cube. He finally did it, but he blew some anger puffs of steam in those weeks. Reese doesn't want to see those anger puffs again right now.

Dean murmurs to himself in a whisper and points back and forth between the two maps. Reese lets him work. She glances around the bison bedroom and wonders who came into the room before. She walks over to the grunting bison on the wall and looks hard at him. "Bison, are we safe right now?" Reese whispers, hoping Dean doesn't hear her. Dean doesn't pause his murmuring, so must not have heard her talk to the wall. The wall bison grunts once. Reese smiles and thanks him. A wave of relief overcomes her knowing that they are safe right now. Ever since they stepped out of the closet, she has wondered whether that big guy would come back. And now they have the map, they have more to protect than just themselves. She thinks about her mom and dad and hopes that they aren't worrying like crazy about them. Reese really misses Tutu and wonders if Tutu misses them. She also wonders about Emma and hopes that the pirates leave them alone.

"Reese, I got it! I think that I figured out this map!" Dean yells. He pumps his fists in the air. The wall bison grunts once. "Thanks, bison buddy!" Dean says with a nod.

"I knew that you would figure it out! Tell me about it," Reese says, walking back over to the bed with the two maps.

Dean smiles back at her and smooths out both maps. "Okay, so you know the national park's name is Erutuf?"

"Yes. What does that have to do with the map?" Reese asks, raising her right eyebrow.

"Everything. What is Erutuf?" Dean asks.

"I have no idea. Maybe the name of the person who donated money for this island?"

"Think about the word." Dean waits for his sister to reply. The room remains silent for a few minutes.

The wall bison grunts three times. Dean and Reese look at each other.

"Are the pirates coming?" Reese asks. The wall bison grunts once. "Should we hide or leave here?" The wall bison grunts twice. "What is two grunts? Should we leave the room?" Reese's voice cracks as her nerves kick into high gear. The bison grunts once. "Should we hide in another room?" The bison grunts once again.

"Thank you, bison buddy," Dean says. The bison grunts one more time.

Dean grabs both maps and folds them up faster than Reese grabs her bag. They run out of the room and pause in the castle's upstairs' hallway. Then they run down the hall and go into the rainbow playroom.

# The Attack

oud bangs come through the castle front doors. Dean and Reese hear a few men arguing about where to go next. Reese points to a large rainbow dollhouse standing about four feet tall. Dean nods, and they run over to it, crawl down to go through the two-feet-tall glittery door, and quickly close the door. Reese sits down on the floor and tries to take a few deep breaths to calm her panic. Dean finds a periscope on the side of the house. He kneels down and places his eyes up to it to watch for the men.

The men's voices grow in volume, and the two children can hear them marching up the stairs. There must be about four or five of them this time. Reese grabs a rainbow pillow and hugs it tight. She closes her eyes and keeps taking deep breaths like in her mom's meditation app.

Dean watches through the periscope. He looks down from the scope and places the maps into Reese's bag. He then tries to cover the maps by stuffing a rainbow blanket from the dollhouse in the bag over them.

A Rainbow Brite doll sits in the other corner of their dollhouse. The doll has blonde yarn hair in a ponytail and wears a space-looking rainbow outfit. A little purple star sits on her left cheek. The dolls were really popular in the 1980s.

The doll shifts and stands up. She walks over to Reese and Dean's corner and stands next to them. "Ahem, can I help you with the pirates?" Rainbow Brite asks Reese. Reese starts to scream in response, but Dean quickly covers her mouth. "I'm so sorry that I startled you. My name is Rainbow Brite. This is my room. We help protect against the pirates like the panda and bison you have already met." Dean and Reese simply stare at the doll in shock. Reese could catch a bird in her mouth because it is open so wide.

"I guess the panda on the wall talks to us, and there is a real talking sea turtle, so why not a doll? Hi, Rainbow Brite," Dean says. He waves to the doll. Reese still stares at the doll without saying a word.

"Hello. Can I help you both with these pirates?"

"Yes, we would love any help. They are almost here," Dean replies.

Reese continues to sit in silence, hugging the rainbow pillow. She keeps her eyes glued to the doll and plans to run fast if it comes any closer. Reese has never been a fan of dolls; she likes stuffed animals more than dolls.

"We need to keep these pirates away from you. The one guy went and got his friends, so they must know that you or someone is in here. You will have to battle them," Rainbow Brite says.

Reese gulps and squeezes her pillow tighter.

Dean's eyes grow big. "How can you help us?" he asks, mustering strength for both Reese and him at the moment.

Rainbow Brite digs under some blankets near where she sat when they first came into the dollhouse. She pulls out two very sparkly, colorful, long, swordlike objects. She walks back to Dean and Reese and hands one to each of them. "These are special weapons for this room, to protect it. Each room has special weapons somewhere in it. You will use these weapons and trust them. Trust yourself and think about protecting the magic of this national park. Get ready— they are almost here." Rainbow Brite walks back over to her corner and goes quiet. She looks like a regular doll now.

"Reese, we need to do this. We need to protect the national park, Emma, and all her friends," Dean says to his sister, who continues to hold the pillow in a death clutch.

Reese nods and takes a deep breath. She places the pillow down next to her. She looks at Rainbow Brite and nods to the doll. The doll smiles back.

"Let's go to battle!" Dean says. He pumps his left fist into the air as he leaves the dollhouse first. Reese takes another deep breath and grips the weapon tightly. She follows Dean out into the playroom. Reese and Dean move to the center of the room and wait a minute before the door flies open.

Five men walk into the playroom and are wearing black tuxedos. They look like they should be at a wedding, not in a rainbow children's playroom. Each man has a different bowtie. Dean tries not to giggle at the five men, who look like penguins to him. He thinks that they should dress tougher than penguins to intimidate people.

The one man with a glittery gray bowtie speaks first. "Hi there, little children. I think that you have something of ours. We will be nice if you just hand it over." He reaches his hand out with his palm up, smiling.

"We don't have anything of yours. We are just playing in this fun room here. Want to play a game with us?" Dean says without smiling back to the man.

"Is this kid serious?" the man with an orange bowtie says to the others.

"Little boy, we know you have it. Give it to us. We don't want to have to play rough," says the glittery, gray bowtie man.

"Why are we being nice and wasting time here? Let's just take it from them. They are just kids," says the man with the red bowtie. He moves up next to the gray bowtie man. "As you can see, boy, some of my friends aren't as nice as me. Just give us what we want."

"What do you want?" Dean asks.

"Seriously? The map, kid. Give us the map."

"We don't have a map," Dean replies. He stands up a little taller.

"What if we're wrong, and they don't have it? They are just kids," says the man with a blue bowtie. He stands closest to the door.

Gray bowtie man swings around to him and says, "They have it. Are you in on this operation or not?" Blue bowtie man goes silent in response and shuffles his feet. The fifth man, with a green bowtie, moves closer to the door.

Gray bowtie man asks Dean for the map one more time. Dean shrugs his shoulders. In a swift movement, Dean grabs a toy blaster lying next him and starts blasting the men. Nerf bullets fly throughout the room in all directions. Reese stands guard next to Dean as he blasts hundreds of these blue nerf bullets, which fly all over the rainbow playroom.

The green bowtie man runs out of the door as if he knew the attack was coming. The door slams shut after he departs. One gone.

The blue bowtie man ducks behind a giant stuffed rainbow to take cover. His body shakes quietly behind the stuffed rainbow.

A nerf bullet nails the orange bowtie man in the eye. He yelps in pain and covers his face. More bullets nail his covered face.

The gray and red bowtie men duck behind two different toys. The red bowtie yells out some adult bad words (the ones that get children sent to the principal's office).

Dean focuses his aim on the gray and red bowtie men, but his blaster slows down. He glances down at it and gulps. There are only a few bullets left in this blaster. He blasts the two remaining men with these last bullets. Then he throws the blaster down and looks at Reese. He nods to their special swords and then to her. She takes a deep breath and nods back.

The red bowtie guy stands up first. He looks taller now for some reason. He pulls something out of his pocket. Reese ducks, and Dean dives to the side. The red man throws the ball in his hand at them. The ball looks like an orange-scented bath bomb, but Reese and Dean know that he wouldn't be throwing a bath bomb at them right now. The orange ball explodes in the air. Orange gases float from the ball as the ball disintegrates like a bath bomb, but with gases. Reese wishes she was in a bath right now, watching the ball turn from the ball shape into just gases in the room.

# The Search

D ean starts coughing. Reese coughs even harder. They both try to cover their faces from the orange gases, but it floats all over the room. It should be the orange room, not the rainbow room. Reese falls to the floor and goes quiet. Dean stops coughing and slumps over.

"What are you doing? We can't harm children." the gray bowtie man yells at the red bowtie man.

"We need the maps, and I got tired of waiting. Let's get the maps and get out of this creepy castle. The annoying kids will be fine. I think," the red bowtie man replies.

"You think? You should know what these gases do before using them. Come on, dude!" says the gray bowtie man.

The orange and blue bowtie men stand there in silence, watching these two.

"I don't think these gases are harmful to kids, but who knows? We have never used it on kids before. Who cares? We will be gone soon. I'll check the boy. You check the girl. You other two, look around the room," says the red bowtie man. He walks over to Dean. Dean remains unconscious and slumped over, holding on to the sword.

The gray bowtie man walks over to Reese, who lies on the floor also unconscious and holding her sword. He looks around her and doesn't see any maps. He tries to take the sword but can't get it out of her hands.

The red bowtie man checks Dean's pockets and doesn't see the maps. He also tries to take Dean's sword, but he can't pull it out of his hands. He kicks Dean in frustration and looks at the others.

The orange and blue bowtie men look around the room. The orange bowtie man flips through a container of Legos. The blue bowtie man gingerly moves some stuffed animals around, looking for the map.

"It has to be in here," says the gray bowtie man. He runs his hand through his short gray hair and moves into the center of the room.

"We have to find the map. We can't fail on this mission," says the orange bowtie man, standing up from his Legos and looking around the room through the orange haze.

"Why didn't this orange stuff make us pass out?" the blue bowtie man asks while reorganizing the stuffed animals.

"I gave you an antidote to it in your breakfast today, in case it was needed," replies the red bowtie man. He walks over to the dollhouse.

"You drugged us?" the blue bowtie man asks in a higher pitch.

"Would you rather be lying on the floor out cold instead, like them? Say thank you. And find the map!" replies the red bowtie man.

"We need to work together right now and find this thing. It has to be in this room," says the gray bowtie man.

The red bowtie man enters the dollhouse. He looks around and sees just a rainbow doll, a few other colorful toys, and blankets. He pauses at the rainbow doll. The doll seems to look back at him but doesn't move. He looks around the house again and feels something going on here.

Dean starts to shift his body and wake up. He opens his eyes and sees three men searching for the maps. Then he sees Reese lying on the floor asleep still. Dean inches his body very slowly over to a large box about a foot away from him. He moves like a turtle to avoid any of the men noticing his movements. Inch by inch, Dean scoots to the box.

The red bowtie man knows something must be in this dollhouse. He feels the energy. It must be the map. Maybe those kids hid it in here?

Dean reaches the large box and goes around on the other side of it. The men can't see him now he is behind this box. He takes a deep breath and tries to remember what happened. He remembers the orange gas, and that's it. Dean knows that the men haven't found the map yet, or they would have left by now.

Reese's eyes flutter open. Then her eyes go wide as she sees the blue bowtie man walk right by her. She freezes her body, closes her eyes fast, and holds her breath. The blue bowtie man moves across the room. She exhales without making any noise. Reese sees Dean waving to her from behind a large box. She nods to him and understands that he wants her to come over there. She looks around the room and spots three of the five men. The three are busy and not near her right now. Reese hops to her feet and darts to the large box.

Dean grabs his sister and hugs her hard. She hugs him back just as hard, grabs his hand, and holds it.

The song "Rainbow Connection" blasts from overhead speakers in the room. Orange bowtie man bumps his head on a colorful play structure because the start of the song surprises him. The blue bowtie man hums along to the song and continues his search, unfazed. The gray bowtie man tries to yell something to the others, but no one can hear him over the loud music.

Reese looks at Dean and says, "Okay, here's our chance to talk, with this loud song playing right now. We need to get the bag in the dollhouse. Should we just make a run for it? I doubt that they have more gas with them."

"I agree that we have to get those maps. Should we make a run for it or try a distraction? We need to use the swords if we battle them," Dean replies. He wonders who turned this song on and where the speakers are in this room.

"This song is pretty distracting!" Reese says. She points to the blue bowtie man, who grabs an American Girl doll and starts dancing the waltz with her and singing to it. Dean tries not to giggle at him, but he can't help it.

"Okay, let's make a run for it into the dollhouse. I'll count, and on five, let's go. Bring your sword," Reese says. Dean nods, and they both get into a runner's takeoff position. The song continues to play at a high volume throughout the room.

"One, two, three, four, and five," says Reese. They take off in a sprint to the dollhouse. Dean enters the house first. Reese crashes into him because he stops right by the door. She soon sees why.

# Sword Magic

"**Well**, well, well. What do we have here? I guess the gas didn't kill you both. I did think that it should have knocked you out longer, though. Where is it?" says the red bowtie man in the dollhouse. The music continues to blast at a high volume in the playroom.

"We aren't going to give you the map. We are here to protect these animals and this national park," Dean says loudly enough for the red bowtie man to hear. He stands up taller, puts out his sword, and leans in, ready for battle.

The red bowtie man laughs and tosses the rainbow doll into the air. Reese jumps up and pulls out her sword too. The red bowtie man keeps laughing. Reese and Dean don't understand his laughter. The man shakes his head and looks at the two children again. "Are you seriously going to battle me?" he asks.

Dean lunges the sword at the man without a word. The sword lights up. Rainbows shoot out of the sword and color the room. A colorful confetti of lights sparkles around the room.

Dean and Reese look at each other and gasp. Both Dean and Reese's clothes have changed. They now have on national park ranger uniforms. Dean and Reese both wear gray shirts, green trouser pants with black belts, and the iconic flat tan hats. Their swords now glow bright with neon rainbow colors.

The red bowtie man lunges at Reese while she looks over her new outfit. He grabs her left wrist and pulls her hard. Reese pumps her right arm with the sword into the air and swings hard at him. The sword hits the red bowtie man in the head. He falls to the ground with a loud lump, and his body glows rainbow. Reese looks at him, smiling. She did it! She feels like Jane Goodall, protecting animals.

Dean hurries to find the bag with the maps in the dollhouse. He moves some blankets, but the bag isn't there. Dean sees a park ranger backpack sitting there. He opens the backpack to find the two maps and all of Reese's other supplies in it. He puts on his new backpack fast and stands up.

"There are at least three more guys out there. We can do it. Let's go, sis!" Dean says to Reese. She smiles and nods.

Dean heads out of the dollhouse first, and Reese follows right behind.

In the dollhouse corner, the Rainbow Brite doll smiles and nods to herself. She picks up a remote and hits a button, which plays the song, "Somewhere Over the Rainbow" by Judy Garland just as loudly as the last song. Rainbow Brite leans back against the dollhouse wall.

Out in the playroom, rainbows continue to shoot out from their swords. The rainbows bounce around and hit toys and the walls. The rainbows appear to dance to the music in some sort of magical rhythm.

Reese spots the blue bowtie man dancing with a new stuffed animal. She creeps over to him and whacks him on the shoulders with her sword. The blue bowtie man flops to the floor, still holding the stuffed animal. He doesn't move, and his eyes close. Like the red bowtie man, his body glows rainbow.

The song plays louder now. "Somewhere over the rainbow, blue birds fly. Birds fly over the rainbow. Why then, oh why can't I?"

Dean spins around and sees the orange bowtie man, who comes running full speed at Dean. Dean sticks out his foot and watches the orange bowtie man trip and fall to the ground. The man yelps in pain and grabs his ankle. Dean lifts up his sword and strikes the orange man's other ankle.

Like the other two pirates, the orange bowtie man passes out, and his body glows rainbow.

"Nice job, brother!" Reese says to him. She gives him a high-five. "Where is the gray one? The scared green one must have left, but I doubt the gray man did. He seems in charge." She looks around the room.

Dean says, "He must be over by those rainbow boxes, searching for the maps. It's so loud in here, that I don't think he's heard any of our fights. Should we get him or just leave with the maps?"

"I think that we should head out now with these maps and get them protected. Our mission is about the maps," Reese says.

"Okay. These battles are fun, though. Let's go."

Dean and Reese walk to the rainbow playroom's door and continue to hold their swords. Dean still has the park ranger backpack on his back. A new song starts to play in the room: "She's a Rainbow" by the Rolling Stones.

Reese places her hand on the doorknob, but someone pulls her hair hard and throws her to the ground. Dean spins around to see the gray bowtie man holding a knife to his sister on the floor.

"Not so fast. Give me the maps, and you get your sister. I know that you have them in your fancy park ranger backpack. I don't want to hurt anyone, but I need those maps."

"Dean, don't give him anything!" Reese squeaks out.

"Why do you need these maps?" Dean asks.

"You don't even know how special these maps are, do you? Stupid kids. Give it to me now. I won't wait long."

The song stops playing midsentence. Silence fills the room, which feels strange after three songs playing repeatedly at maximum volume. All three of them look around the room, trying to figure out the music.

Dean looks at Reese and gives one nod. Reese nods back. Dean yells, "Rangers!" as loudly as he can. Reese squirms away from the gray bowtie man and hops to her feet. The gray bowtie man looks confused as Dean and Reese lunge at him at the same time with their swords. The gray bowtie man can't react that fast and falls to the playroom floor after the two swords touch him. Just like the other pirates, the gray bowtie man's body glows rainbow.

# Celebration

Dean hugs his sister hard and long. After he releases her from the hug, they look around the room and watch in silence. The dancing rainbow lights stop. The Nerf bullets from their first attack vanish. The bodies of the pirates disappear. Their clothes return to normal as the park ranger uniforms vanish. Last, their magical, colorful swords disappear from their hands.

"That was so epic!" Dean says with a huge smile.

"Crazy! Hey, I've got a great idea where to hide the maps. Let's get out of here, just in case they come back," Reese replies.

"Lead the way, sister. Hey, I still have the park ranger backpack. That's cool!"

Dean and Reese leave the rainbow playroom and head down the sandcastle stairs. Reese leads Dean outside and along the beach. After some time walking along the beach, they find the original tree where they saw the tourist family. Reese spots a hidden canister and points to it. Dean takes the map out of his backpack. He places the secret one into the canister and puts the park brochure back into his backpack. They hide the canister and leave the area.

"It's like leaving a geocache here," Dean says. Reese agrees that it feels more like geocaching now that the pirates are gone.

Dean and Reese walk toward the ocean. The cool wind and warm sun feel good on their faces after their battles inside the castle. Dean and Reese sit on a log and dip their feet into the ocean water as it goes back and forth.

"Elf boy and Reese, you did it!" squeaks a sea turtle from the water.

"Emma!" Reese squeals. She jumps up, runs over to her, and hugs the turtle. Dean shakes his head and smiles at Emma.

"We are grateful to you both. You have helped all the animals of Erutuf National Park. We cannot thank you enough," Emma says to them.

"Can I ask you a question, Emma?" Reese asks, twirling her hair.

"Sure."

"What does Erutuf mean? The name for this national park. I looked at the brochure, and it doesn't explain it."

"It means Future. In fact, Erutuf is the word *future* spelled backward. This national park stands to protect the future of our climate by protecting all of the animals, landscapes, climates, and wonders of our world," Emma explains.

Reese says, "That's so amazing! I wish that we could see the whole national park."

"What does the map that we protected lead to, then?" Dean asks. He feels slightly disappointed that they didn't get to go check it out.

"I guess that I should tell you, because you helped us so much. The map leads to a magical stash of elixir. The elixir provides all the magic here for this special national park. Without the magic elixir, the national park would not survive. Each area in the national park has its own map and its own stash of this elixir."

"Why would pirates want that? Don't they usually want money, gold, or jewelry?" Dean asks.

Emma replies, "Remember that these are special pirates. These pirates want the elixir to sell on the black market to make tons of money."

"Wow. This place is so cool! We are so honored to have helped it!" Reese says. Strong confidence flows from her voice.

"Man, I wish I could have followed the map and then seen the elixir!" Dean says. He kicks some sand.

"Once again, we can't thank you enough. And it is now time for you to return to your home and family," Emma says.

Dean and Reese both hug her tight. "We will miss you all here," Dean says. Reese fights back tears and nods at Dean's words.

"Elf boy, I sure like you. And Miss Reese, I like you too. Now, let's get you back home to dance your tutu."

"It's our dog, not a dance," Dean says giggling. Reese smiles.

"And am I an elf?" Emma says, smirking.

"We will miss you lots!" Reese chokes out. She is still fighting the tears welling up in her eyes.

"Okay, let's walk over to this spot. Close your eyes and think about turtles swimming in the ocean," Emma instructs Dean and Reese. Dean and Reese follow her instructions and close their eyes. They start to hear ballet music. They see the beautiful sea turtles gliding around the blue ocean waters. The ocean colors start to swirl faster and faster.

# Home

Lick, lick, and lick. The hot, wet tongue tickles Dean's cheeks.

"Emma, are you licking me?" Dean asks as he opens his eyes. "Tutu!" He gives Tutu a huge hug and wrestles her to the ground with him.

Reese opens her eyes and sees her brother wrestling their dog on the ground. "Dean, we are home!" Tutu runs over and jumps up on Reese. Reese giggles and kisses Tutu on her furry head.

"Yes, silly sister, we are home. Did we really go to Erutuf National Park?"

"I think so. You remember it all, right? I miss Emma."

"Duh, I remember it. I miss it all too. I miss hearing that elf voice." Dean smiles, reaches over his shoulder, and touches a park ranger backpack. "Reese, I still have the backpack!"

"Cool. You need a new one anyway, for school."

Dean points to the clock next to the television. "Look at the clock. We haven't missed any time here. That's so cool! We time-traveled or something!"

"So crazy!" Reese replies.

Dean and Reese run off to find their parents and give them both big hugs. The parents don't understand the spontaneous affection, but they don't refuse the hugs.

After a few days of regular life back at home, Dean and Reese relax on the sofa with Tutu at their feet on the carpet. Tutu groans with happiness as Reese pets her softly.

"Hey, I think that becoming a junior park ranger has a new meaning now, when we go to national parks," Dean says. He smiles at his sister while remembering their adventures.

"Yes, but I think that watching videos online has a new meaning! Let's watch another video." Reese reaches for her tablet.

"Sounds fun! I want to watch one about bison," Dean says. Reese enters it into the search engine. Dean and Reese smirk at each other while the website loads the video options. Tutu jumps up on the sofa to check out their next adventure.

A new video of bison roaming an open valley loads up, and ballet music starts to play.

# Acknowledgements

Thank you to Danielle Borst, Nailah Khatri, Jeff Slone, and all the great editorial, illustration, design, and marketing teams at Archway Publishing, a division of Simon & Schuster. Thank you to all my beta readers for taking the time to read the various drafts of this book and offer feedback. Thank you to the SCBWI organization and allies for providing suggestions and guidance on this crazy path of writing and publishing. Thank you to Gage Bock for guiding me to stretch and go beyond my comfort zone. Thank you to Dr. J. Patrick Murphy for empowering students that it's all about the mission. Thank you for helping enhance my writing skills, especially with that pesky passive voice. Thank you to Neal Desai for inspiring us all to live life to its fullest. Thank you to Jesse Bennett for advocating for a fellow local author.

Thank you to Ginger Bernard for adventuring out in a pandemic to make a camera-shy person look good in a photo and for all the pep talks.

Thank you to all of my mom friends for all their support, laughs, book recommendations, wine, and cheers.

Thank you to the HH crew for providing comfort, relief, and laughs during a pandemic and also for their meaningful friendships.

Thank you to my parents for all of their encouragement and love. Thank you for valuing the importance of a solid education and giving me opportunities to grow. Thank you for your examples of hard work and public service over all these years.

Thank you to Christy Feinberg for your advice and guidance on book publishing, your creative inspiration, and your confidence in me. Thank you for always offering a world of colorful glitter and for always being there for me.

A big thank you to my children, Carter and Kaitlyn, for sparking the creation a magical place for you to explore. Thank you for being my biggest fans! You two are the best kids in the world and love you both tons!

A special thank you to my husband, Steve, for an introduction to the magic of our national parks. And thank you for encouraging me to find my magic back in our early days together - writing on the riverbanks while you enjoyed fly fishing. Thank you for still encouraging it many years and two children later. Have I told you how great you are yet today?

Made in United States
Orlando, FL
03 January 2022

12757088R00071